WINGS IN THE WILD

Also by Margarita Engle

* also available in Spanish

* *Enchanted Air:*
Two Cultures, Two Wings: A Memoir

The Firefly Letters:
A Suffragette's Journey to Cuba

* *Forest World*

Hurricane Dancers:
The First Caribbean Pirate Shipwreck

Jazz Owls:
A Novel of the Zoot Suit Riots

The Lightning Dreamer:
Cuba's Greatest Abolitionist

* *Lion Island:*
Cuba's Warrior of Words

The Poet Slave of Cuba:
A Biography of Juan Francisco Manzano

* *Rima's Rebellion:*
Courage in a Time of Tyranny

Silver People:
Voices from the Panama Canal

* *Soaring Earth:*
A Companion Memoir to Enchanted Air

* *The Surrender Tree:*
Poems of Cuba's Struggle for Freedom

Tropical Secrets:
Holocaust Refugees in Cuba

The Wild Book

* *With a Star in My Hand:*
Rubén Darío, Poetry Hero

* *Your Heart, My Sky:*
Love in a Time of Hunger

WINGS IN THE WILD

MARGARITA ENGLE

atheneum

New York London Toronto Sydney New Delhi

A

atheneum

An imprint of Simon & Schuster Children's Publishing Division
1230 Avenue of the Americas, New York, New York 10020
Text © 2023 by Margarita Engle
Jacket illustration © 2023 by Gaby D'Alessandro
Jacket design by Rebecca Syracuse © 2023 by Simon & Schuster, Inc.
For information about special discounts for bulk purchases, please contact Simon & Schuster Special Sales
at 1-866-506-1949 or business@simonandschuster.com.
The Simon & Schuster Speakers Bureau can bring authors to your live event. For more information or to
book an event, contact the Simon & Schuster Speakers Bureau at 1-866-248-3049 or visit our website at
www.simonspeakers.com.
Interior design by Rebecca Syracuse
The text for this book was set in Bembo Book MT Pro.
Manufactured in the United States of America
First Edition
2 4 6 8 10 9 7 5 3 1
Library of Congress Cataloging-in-Publication Data
Names: Engle, Margarita, author.
Title: Wings in the wild / Margarita Engle.
Description: First edition. | New York : Atheneum Books for Young Readers, 2023. | Audience: Ages
12 up. | Summary: When a hurricane exposes Soleida's family's secret sculpture garden, the Cuban
government arrests her artist parents, forcing her to escape alone to Central America where she meets
Dariel, a Cuban American boy, and together they work to protect the environment and bring attention
to the imprisoned artists in Cuba.
Identifiers: LCCN 2022004266 | ISBN 9781665926362 (hardcover) |
ISBN 9781665926386 (ebook)
Subjects: CYAC: Novels in verse. | Environmentalism—Fiction. | Refugees—Fiction. | Artists—Fiction. |
Political prisoners—Fiction. | Protest movements—Fiction. | Cuban Americans—Fiction. |
Cuba—Fiction. | LCGFT: Novels in verse. | Romance fiction.
Classification: LCC PZ7.5.E54 Wig 2023 | DDC [Fic]—dc23
LC record available at https://lccn.loc.gov/2022004266

para los caminantes cubanos
y los costarricenses generosos

and for tree planters
and wing dreamers
everywhere

We plant seeds in the ground
and dreams in the sky.

Alberto Ríos

CONTENTS

TOCORORO-GIRL

Soleida

age 16

Cuba

2018

Aviary

Winged beings are meant to be free,
not caged.

At the heart of our dilapidated seaside home
in the central courtyard—hidden by walls—
we have a secret museum of living statues
carved from the growing limbs
of richly hued native trees.

Deep reddish-brown mahogany like my skin,
midnight-black ebony like my eyes, and radiant
golden majagua like my sunny name.

This last tree is a wild hibiscus
with yellow flowers that attract
tiny emerald zunzunes
and their minuscule cousins
los zunzuncitos, this island's endemic
bee hummingbirds, the smallest pajaritos
on Earth, found nowhere else, just Cuba.
¡Ay, Cuba! How we suffer here, surrounded
by imprisoned beauty.

Art Crimes

The problem with our sculpture garden
is that the statues are illegal.

Mami and Papi are dissidents—protesters
who crave
artistic liberty.

Visiting birds come and go freely
by zooming high above the coral stone walls
but we
are in a cage
imposed by Ley 349,
a decree that bans any art
that protests the banning
of art.

Carved Wingbeats

The tocororo is Cuba's national bird.
Blue, white, and red, like our flag.
He perches and flicks his tail
back and forth
in a dance
of love.

Everyone knows that los tocororos
cannot survive in captivity.
That is why, each time I pose
as the inspiration for his sculpted form
I feel like a symbol
of liberty.

Winged, rooted, and chained,
my tocororo-self tries to fly
but always fails.

Only freedom of expression for artists
will transform these statues.
Only then will my parents cut the carved chains
that keep my winged image from soaring.

Neighbors

Only our closest vecinos know
about the garden of secret art.
They're a sweet middle-aged couple
named Liana and Amado, who—when
they were my age—became local heroes
by teaching everyone how to farm
during the island's most tragic time of hunger.

Now they raise an ancient breed of singing dogs
whose chants we hear day and night, releasing
a musical miracle of hope.

The dogs, like el tocororo, are endemic
to this island, and like el tocororo,
their music cannot be caged.
They need to sing freely
along with Liana and Amado's daughter,
a musical girl who loves to serenade
every winged being, sea creature,
and four-footed land animal she sees.
Her voice always gives me a warm shiver
that makes me think angels might be listening.

Transformation

Liana is the one who told me the legend
of Tocororo and Atabey, our Taíno goddess
of water, moon, and Earth.

When a girl called Tocororo
was captured by invaders
Atabey freed her
by turning her
into a bird.

Now, every time I pose for a chained tocororo statue,
I think of that bird-girl—did she miss her human self
or was she thrilled, drumming the air with new wings?

Liana says large birds like geese and swans
can get stuck in small ponds if they don't have
enough room to run on the surface of the water,
flapping to build the momentum
for flight.

When You Grow Up in the Home of Artists . . .

you learn that it is impossible to imagine
life without imagination
so you keep
imagining
the day
when
police
will discover
your parents'
artistic crimes
and you wonder
if posing is as illegal
as sculpting

How It Feels to Be Carved

Tree rings are the fingerprints of time
gathering themselves into the wood
where my sculpted wings

grow.

Rescuing Winged Beings

I can't protect myself from the art police
so instead I rescue birds—real ones,
not statues—zunzunes y zunzuncitos
tocororos y cartacubas—this last
a brightly hued little creature
that looks like a hummingbird
but nests in mud tunnels
and hunts insects
instead of sipping
delicate nectar.

Every one of the winged orphans I feed
is a member of a unique, endemic species
found nowhere else on Earth,
only on this island
of my ancestors,
people who believed
in transformations.

Rescuing Wingless Beings

Sometimes after school
I sit and watch polimita tree snails
climb
all over
the statues
of my winged
and chained
bird-girl-self.

The tree snails have been painted by nature
with swirls of lemon, orange, guava-pink, coffee-brown,
and creamy white like the insides of coconuts.
Polimitas are so beautiful that tourists
kill them by seizing their shells
as souvenirs.

They're endangered, so whenever I see one
outside our garden walls, I bring it in to keep it
hidden
safe
secret.

Stormy Shore

Today the wind is ferocious.
A hurricane is approaching.

I'm a wildlife rescuer,
but who will
rescue
me?

A World of Catastrophes

censorship
danger
art police

hurricanes
climate crisis
extinction of species

my imagination
needs a place of refuge
from constant
terror

Bittersweet Sixteen

I should be free
to dream
of a boy
a hug
a kiss

maybe
someday
soon

Midnight

shrieking demon-wind
rearing dragon waves

our   roof   flies   away
my   room   sinks   and   floats

garden walls
gone

only the statues
on deeply rooted trees
remain

visible
our outlawed art
exposed

We Swim

frantically
splash
churn
pray

neighbors
are homeless too

no one
has any place
to seek refuge

our whole town
is part of the rising sea
every man-made structure
ruined

the revenge of nature
for a climate torment
ignored

Hilltop

From here, we have a view of soldiers
arriving to help evacuate storm victims.

When the uniformed men and women
see our sculptures, they shake their heads,
and we know we've been identified
as outlaws.

How long will it be
until art police
arrive
to destroy
the sculptures
then arrest
the sculptors
and their model . . . ?

Rescued

Liana and Amado find us.
Their singing dogs hum quietly.
Their daughter sings peacefully.
My shoulders shiver mysteriously
despite the air's steaming heat.

We follow our neighbors to a cave.
They promise to send us to the city,
where other censored artists
will surely help us
escape.

I've Always Known We Might Have to Flee

sooner or later

but still I mourn

this loss

of my real self

the one who lives

in a garden

of rooted

wings

We Ride through Darkness
in a Horse-Drawn Cart

I feel like a mermaid
clothes still sopping wet
legs and arms exhausted
from swimming
and hiking
mind unaccustomed
to thoughts of exile
in a distant land.

Which country will accept us?
Hardly any nation in the world
grants visitors' visas to Cubans
because they're afraid
we'll stay.

The Book of Exiled Cousins

My parents recite the unwritten list of names
addresses
phone numbers
countries.

Each primo who left the island
had an urgent reason to flee.

Punishment for belief in God back in the '60s,
persecution of artists, poets, and singers,
then hunger in the '90s—
by now we have relatives in Venezuela,
Ecuador, Costa Rica, Spain, Sweden, Miami,
Hialeah, Homestead, Orlando, and Coral Gables.

Will any of them remember us
after so many years in havens
they found when they
were the refugees?

We Choose a Cousin to Trust . . .

Vivi, my mother's prima.
She's a poet, but also a doctor
traded by Cuba to Venezuela
in exchange for petroleum
to keep lights on in our island's
luxury hotels for foreign tourists.

Obediently, I recite Vivi's address
at a clinic in a city called Barquisimeto
near la frontera de Colombia—a city known
as la Ciudad de la Música.

Always choose a place you can leave easily,
my parents admonish.
Are Mami and Papi suddenly treating me
like an adult?

There's also Mireya, una artista in Costa Rica,
but I refuse to memorize more numbers after I hear
my mother warn: just in case we're ever separated.

No, no, no, I refuse to imagine such a horrifying
possibility.

Sixteen is not old enough
to wander the world
without parents.

I won't allow it to happen.
Separation
is not
an option.

We've chosen a name—
Vivi in Venezuela—
and that's where we'll go
and we'll stay
with her
forever.

No more departures.
No more goodbyes to gardens
of rooted wings.

Disguise

An artist in Havana covers my face
with stage makeup so I won't look so young.

He gives me a fake passport that claims
I'm an eighteen-year-old Canadian.

I wear a straight blond wig, comfortable shoes,
sporty clothes, and a jade-green backpack
filled with underwear, T-shirts, a phone,
and a bit of cash.

Everyone knows that this is exactly how
the old bearded tyrant's own daughter escaped
long ago, disguised as a tourist.

El barbudo is dead now, and things
were supposed to improve, but instead
Ley 349 just makes artistic lives worse
and worse.

Las Damas de Blanco

On the way to the airport
we pass a plaza where women
in flowing
white dresses
hold bouquets of graceful
white blossoms
and handwritten signs
showing the names
of husbands, sons, brothers, and fathers,
mothers, daughters, sisters, and cousins
imprisoned as punishment for painting
writing
singing
or sculpting
something
illegal.

Aeropuerto Internacional José Martí

By the time I pass through a metal detector
and luggage inspection, I already feel foreign
in this airport named for Cuba's most beloved
nineteenth-century poet, who was arrested
when he was my age for the crime
of writing a poem with lyrics
about liberty.

He grew up and set Cuba free from Spain
even though it meant sacrificing his own life
along the way.

If he were alive now, Martí would once again be
in danger of becoming one of the prisoners
remembered only by las damas de blanco
the women in white
with their devotion
to the recitation of names
of los desaparecidos
who disappear
into prison cells
forever.

Airplanes Have Always Seemed Mythical

suddenly, strangely, incredibly
I'm about to be transformed
into a shape-shifter
ready to zoom
away
wings
real

Separated

Mami and Papi
were right behind me!
Where are they?

Frantically, I peer through the tiny
airplane window, and there they stand
on the black tarmac
surrounded by policía.

Handcuffs.
They're prisoners . . .

      so that's it, my nightmare in daylight
      now I'm on this flight alone
      unless I rush out and take my place
      beside them
            but
            I
            don't
            because they made me promise
                        to flee
                and I am obedient.

Guilt in Midair

Birds can soar only because their bones
are hollow, filled with the lightness of air
instead of dense marrow.

My own skeleton must be made of stone
because I feel so incredibly heavy with shame
as I peer at a window-shaped patch
of sky.

First Mami and Papi in chains.
Now clouds below, sun above,
and everything else so impossible.

Did I really leave them?
I should have rushed back out
to accept my place in a prison cell
or out on la plaza, dressed in white,
carrying flowers.

How can I be selfish enough to soar away
from everyone I've ever
loved?

SONG-BOY

Dariel

age 16

California

2018

With a Guitar in My Hands

I feel natural
holding this hourglass-shaped
wooden box of air and sound
made by Abuelo from trees
on the island, back when he
was cubano instead of
Cuban-American.

No hyphen.
No separation.
No bridge.
Just wholeness.
It's a state of mind I'll never know.
I've always felt oddly divided.
The Miami half of our family
listens to politicians, but I'm
a forest dweller in a canyon
of dying oaks and pines, the trees
dried by drought and pierced by beetles,
this drumming of hungry woodpeckers
the hollow rhythm
for my songs.

Feeling

I don't know why birds and animals
always gather around every time I sing
in the old Cuban style known as filin,
love songs as gentle as lullabies
filled with emotion
and yearning.

Scrub jays, mockingbirds, mourning doves,
squirrels, lizards, a family of raccoons . . .

Abuelo says it means I have the Taíno talent
for storytelling, my voice giving warm shivers
to anyone who understands nature.

I concentrate so intensely on serenading
the assembly of wild forest creatures
that I almost fail to notice this dreaded
odor
of smoke.

Chased by Flames

I stand, move, run,
follow alarmed animals,
guitar still strapped over my shoulder,
car keys, phone, buttons—punch 911!
Why didn't I have it on speed dial?
I race, open gates, release the neighbors'
livestock and pets—frantic,
I lift
and toss
two labradoodles
three pygmy goats
and a kitten
into the back seat.

Horses, birds, and wild creatures
have already escaped.

Inside the car, I sing to calm
all my four-legged passengers.

Blistered

I should have worn gloves
or wrapped my hands in my shirt.

The latches of the gates were already scalding.
Now my fingertips on the steering wheel
feel like exposed nerves
screeching.

The stench of gloom
       and taste of ash
            are left behind
       as I peel rubber
around curves
    down   down   downhill
until
we
     reach
firefighters
        who guide me
          toward separate shelters
            for animals and people.

Shelter

dogs in kennels
goats corralled
kitten cuddled
neighbors grateful
parents on their way
from a Hollywood gala
their insurance agent
and architect
already contacted
to start rebuilding
the woodland mansion
that keeps our family hidden
from adoring fans and paparazzi
who haunt us as if my parents'
soap opera characters were real
meanwhile my scorched fingers
are treated and soothed
by medical volunteers
but blistered thoughts
can't be healed
with ointments

or painkillers
no way to swallow
flame-scarred anger
and make my explosive
climate rage
vanish

Climate Justice

Climate arson should be an international crime.
Ecocide needs to be punishable, just like genocide
or torture, because this feels like a battle
against greed,
the owners
of corporations
and presidents of nations
unwilling to face our global
twenty-first century
fragility.

If lawmakers were young enough
to hope they might be alive in the year 2100,
would they treat Earth more gently
or just blast away
in spaceships?

Useful

The shelter is crowded with all sorts of people,
ranging from my school friends to gardeners,
maids, construction workers, and teachers,
so I force myself to stand, move, take action,
offer to help
by using
bandaged fingers
to hand out food, water,
cots, blankets, even books
brought by a retired librarian
who tells me there's no need
to ever feel
useless.

Sparks

The blackened skeleton of our house shows up
on the news, with the headline "Hot Telenovela Stars"
and a story about my parents' exciting
new roles in an English-language
superhero blockbuster film
and the way their home
went up in flames
while their super-cool
genius teenage son
sang to wild animals.

There's a photo of me with the caption
"Just as Hot as Dad"—so that means
paparazzi were out there in the canyon
when the fire started, maybe they even
tossed cigarettes into the parched woods,
but almost as bad, the next photo shows me
carrying a cute kitten,
and the caption is a sarcastic joke—
"Wildlife Whisperer."

It wouldn't take many more pictures
like this

to send me
    into a fury
        of fists
or insults.

If animals
flock to my music,
that's a mystery,
not a comedy . . .

and if I'm such a genius,
I should have known
that sleazy photographers
were hovering around me
like evil drones.

Still, our fire is only one of so many right now.
California is shaped like a torch on the map,
and that's how it's behaving, every dying
drought-stricken forest just one of thousands
of climate change tragedies
ignored by politicians.

The Greta Effect

I need to get away.
We'll soon have a fancy new house,
but luxury doesn't make sense.

No more private jets
to visit Abuelo in Miami.
I don't want a seat in coach either
on a crowded plane that spews pollution
and is full of people who might
recognize me from the few times
I let my parents talk me into
singing for episodes of celebrity
talk shows, and that one day
when I foolishly agreed
to appear on their telenovela
as a magician who communicates
with animals instead of people.

Climate action.
That's what I crave.
Greta Thunberg's Friday Strike.
I'll walk out of school, make adults listen,

remind them that our future
depends on reversing the climate crisis
they still refer to as a bit of a change
instead of an utter disaster.

I'll work hard, graduate super-early,
maybe even wait for college
until I've decided how to help
cool the air
above the suffering surface
of our burning planet
Madre Tierra
Mother Earth.

Mom and Dad expect me to attend
an Ivy League school or music academy,
but I might apply to UC Davis instead
for regenerative agriculture
or environmental forestry
or veterinary medicine
or wildlife biology . . .

A Field Guide to the Cubans of Costa Rica

When I call Abuelo, he says he's writing
a book about los caminantes, the Cubans
who fly to South America, then walk
across farms and jungles before getting
stranded in northern Costa Rica at the border
of Nicaragua, a country that won't let them cross.

Tons of cubanos have been stuck there
for the past couple of years—at least
eight thousand, maybe more.

Abuelo was a persecuted musician in Cuba
until he came to the US by way of Costa Rica
on the Mariel-era airlift, right before the huge
Mariel Boatlift of 1980, and he lived there
for quite a few years, with Abuela and Dad
until the US finally gave them permission
to move to Miami.

Now this book is his way of returning
to the first place that gave his family
a refuge—Costa Rica, not Florida.

How Long Will We Be Gone?

Abuelo invites me to go with him
after my early graduation, in winter
instead of spring.

When I ask how long we'll be away,
he answers with an island-style riddle,
rounding things off to maybe a month,
a year, or forever.

I'll have to fly, but I'll buy carbon credits
to relieve my conscience, and it will be
a chance to see reforestation projects
in the country that pioneered
agroforestry, planting coffee
in the shade of native trees
instead of wiping out
all the natural
wildlife habitat.

Abuelo was a migrant worker
on those coffee farms, sleeping
out in the cloud forest, singing
with monkeys and birds.

Later, in the US, he became
a musicology professor, but as soon as
he retired, he started reminiscing about
his life in the forest, where music
was born
as early humans
listened.

He reminisces about Abuela too.
They were both young in Costa Rica
and Dad was just a little kid
who loved to act out roles
he invented, playing all the parts
in his own plays about animals,
insects, and birds.

BORDER ZONE

Soleida and Dariel

lowland rain forest,
northern Costa Rica

February 2019

Refugee Camp
Soleida

By the time I reach the wide river
that separates Costa Rica from Nicaragua
        I already know
        I won't
          be allowed
            to cross.

No country wants me
so I languish in one more tent
hoping for a miracle
my fake passport
lost or stolen months ago
along with the phone, cash,
and most of my emotions.

The tocororo-girl who escaped sculpted chains
has now shape-shifted into a slow tree snail
silent, wingless,
waiting.

Pity at First Sight
Dariel

Nicaragua won't let Cubans in
but Costa Rica doesn't deport them
because of human rights violations
on the island, so refugees wait in jungle camps
by the thousands, hoping for some way to reach
El Salvador or Guatemala, any country
where los caminantes can keep walking
even though they know
they might not make it
past Mexico,
and if they do
kids and teens
get locked up in cages
by our racist US president
who acts like a brutal dictator . . .

but how could this bald, silent, traumatized girl
walk all the way from South America?
She doesn't even look strong enough
to stand up, and she barely speaks.

Why Should I Talk to Strangers?
Soleida

Interview?
A book?
What good
will it do?
No one
cares.

She Says My Name Scares Her
Dariel

Dariel is too much like Darién,
the roadless jungle in southern Panama
where she lost her cousin while they both
were walking.

Abuelo tries to explain that he chose my name
by combining Mariel, a place of escape,
with los dorados, the golden fish
he imagined must be leaping
far below his family
as they soared away
from the island
in an airplane
back in 1980.

Qué va, Soleida says, the most Cuban response
I can imagine, a phrase old islanders use
to mean "Well, what can you do? It's just
how life is, stuff happens, that sucks."

I've never heard anyone but a cubano
fit entire paragraphs of frustration
into those two short syllables.

When I offer to let Soleida give me
a nickname, she shakes her stubbled head,
falls silent, and closes her big, dark eyes
as if she's already worn out
from the effort of saying
so little.

He Looks Familiar
Soleida

something
about the thick black hair
cinnamon skin and deep turquoise eyes
that remind me of the sea where it's
streaked blue and green

he resembles that actor
en la telenovela, the one
Mami and I always admired
together

maybe I'll get used to his strange name
but I don't think I can ever feel relaxed
while being reminded of memories
from my family
and home

Azabache
Dariel

Her eyes seem as dark as the onyx
every Cuban-American child wears
to ward off evil curses cast by strangers,
but in my advanced-placement genetics class
the teacher said there's no such thing
as truly black human eyes.

Either way, Soleida makes me think of azabache,
the good-luck stones on a bracelet that Mom
made me keep until I was five
in school
getting
teased
for wearing
jewelry.

Now the memory of azabache feels comforting.
It's an island thing, even though I've never been
to Cuba.

I Can Imagine What He Must Think of Me
Soleida

my shaved head
all the dark curls gone

my lean body
all those lost curves
of flesh

I must look
like a shipwrecked ghost
instead of a stranded walker

Music
Dariel

It's my most honest way
to communicate, but what if animals
surround me, and Soleida gets frightened
by the weirdness?

Most people don't understand
that I'm singing *with*
the creatures,
not *to*
them.

Below and Above
Soleida

I feel like I'm underwater.
I wish I'd drowned sooner,
during the hurricane,
or later, in that flash flood
when Vivi was swept away
                              forever.

She was the one who deserved to live.
She kept me walking with her poetry,
helping me match my aching steps
to the rhythm—blistered feet, broken boots,
and every other hardship forgotten
at least for one   moment.

Every time I said I was too tired or too sore
to keep going, she reminded me to look up
and see wild birds in free sky, serenading
                              the future.

Mesmerized
Dariel

She stares.
Those eyes.

My fingers.
These flame-scars.
Does she pity me the same way I pity her
for being homeless and stateless,
unwanted by any nation?

Tonight I'll play the guitar
so she'll see how easily my damaged hands
can still move with a rhythm, a melody, mysterious.

For now I'm motionless in this jungle heat,
daydreaming new lyrics especially for her,
even though she probably doesn't
care about
words.

Full Belly
Soleida

If I were a normal girl I might be attracted,
but right now all I can concentrate on is eating
more and more food, so freely available, mounds
of rice and black beans that I think of as arroz congrí
even though los costarricenses call it gallo pinto—
spotted rooster—and they call themselves ticos
and they keep saying "pura vida"
even though nothing about life
feels pure.

For months Vivi and I picked termites
out of rotten logs, to gobble them because
they were the only protein that was easy
to catch, probably not poisonous,
and unlikely
to bite us.

Guitar Experiment
Dariel

Moonlight.
Night birds, owls,
potoos, bats, and moths, too,
then mammals—kinkajous,
a tamandua, spider monkeys,
and howlers, all attracted
to nocturnal music
the way I'm drawn
to you.

Yes, you, Soleida, as you reach
to touch the island trees this guitar
came from when Abuelo was carving
its shape, fitting the strings,
filling it with his voice
of belief
in love.

Mystified
Soleida

The whoosh and whir of feathers
a thump and tremor of animal feet,
people too, no one can stay away
when you sing
odd boy
your voice
a magnet
making me
long to listen
forever.

What Next?
Dariel

After my first song
all the other refugees
start calling me maestro
while Abuelo smiles proudly
and Soleida says
nothing.

I can't tell if she understands
that I have no control over the animals
and birds who flock to this guitar.

I don't know if she thinks
I'm a magician
or crazy.

Uprooted
Soleida

The wooden mosaic
of his mysterious guitarra
is from my island.

I want to stroke the mahogany, ebony,
and majagua, all the same trees that we grew
and turned into sculptures in our garden,
of winged beings who were free to fly,
carrying me away on the feathers
of daydreams. . . .

Homesickness
overwhelms me.

I don't know if the dancing air that ripples
back and forth between the song-boy and me
is pure sound, or a fountain of memory.

Can la música heal me,
or have I merely been sculpted
all over again?

ARRIVALS

Dariel and Soleida

Caribbean coast, northern Costa Rica

March 2019

Lost in Translation
Dariel

Soon the dry season will end
and rainy heat will overtake us,
turning everything to mud.

We've been in this camp for a month
welcomed by everyone except Soleida,
who just can't seem to speak
about anything
beyond
her plea
for help
finding a lost cousin
and news of her parents
and the location of another
older cousin called Mireya,
an artist whose surname
she can't remember.

She says she has relatives in Florida too
but no addresses or phone numbers,
just fantasies.

I don't know why she won't talk to either
me or Abuelo.
My Spanish is pretty good.
We've always traveled for telenovela episodes
filmed on location, so I've lived for a few weeks
or even months in just about every part
of Latin America
except Cuba.

That's the thing about Cuban-Americans.
We're either hopping back and forth to la isla
loaded with gifts, or we stay away completely,
afraid we'll disappoint los primos by being unable
to deliver the only thing they really want—
permission to enter the United States.

Abuelo says maybe Soleida will agree
to be interviewed if we move to some other
setting, a mountain or a beach, where she
won't feel trapped in this camp.

So he talks to the Costa Rican officials,
and they let him plan a day away
from sorrow.

Turtle Beach
Soleida

Our local guide is some sort of wildlife angel
hired by her government to guard sea turtles
while they lay their eggs and then protect
the nests, so poachers won't sell eggs
to overseas restaurants
and other vendors
of curiosities.

La arribada.
The arrival.
Thousands of females
lumber away from holes
in the sand, where they cover
their eggs, expecting normalcy.

They're like doves, always returning
to their own birthplace when the time
is just right.

They must have maps in their brains
to guide them home from distant depths.

Normalcy No Longer Exists
Dariel

The guide says she might have to move
some of the eggs into an incubator
with a controlled temperature.

Turtles are cold-blooded.
Global warming is turning
too many of the hatchlings
into females.

Within a few decades
they might not be able
to find mates.

Imagine turtles circling the world's oceans
in search of a future for their next generation.

Troubled, I start to hum, and a seagull lands
on my hand, then a row of pelicans approaches,
followed by vultures, ospreys, and caracaras,
all the raptors that will gobble hatchlings
as soon as the eggs open.

When the guide isn't watching,
Abuelo tells me to stop singing
or we'll attract a crowd of people
who might recognize me as my dad's son.

The last thing we need out here
is a video that could bring too many footsteps
crushing nests.

It's all such a riddle.
I didn't even bring my guitar.
There must be a quirk in my voice,
something magical and scientific
at the same time.

Soleida shivers in this heat.
I've read that there are people
who are affected that way by music
because they have a different sort
of wiring in their brains.

Between the two of us
we're both really weird
mysteries.

Odysseys
Soleida

each egg
is a question

each journey a past
linked to the unknown future

if the song-boy and his abuelo
agree to tell their stories
maybe I'll share mine

it's almost a relief to think that Vivi and I
might end up in a book read by strangers someday
when nothing I feel now matters
unless it's remembered
by someone else

if reptiles can evolve into birds
then anything is possible

Wishfulness
Dariel

I told Abuelo this wouldn't work.
Soleida is just as miserable here
as anywhere else, even though
she's starting to look more normal
with short hair almost curling
and the shadows of curves
emerging above and below
her waist, making her look
more human
and more Cuban.

I offer her a protein bar.
She shakes her head.
So I take a bite,
then set the rest on top
of my backpack
and sit here wishing
I'd brought my guitar,
but it might have disrupted
this amazing migration
of ocean creatures. . . .

After Laughter
Soleida

I try to warn Dariel
that he can't eat on a beach
where there are monkeys
but he doesn't pay attention.
He nibbles weird food
of seeds and nuts, then sets it down,
and a moment later, a capuchin
leaps from a sea grape branch,
seizes the protein bar, and races
up the beach, where he gobbles
like a child, barely chewing
before swallowing.

I chuckle at Dariel's surprised expression,
but the act of laughing feels so unnatural
that I stop and remind myself—I don't
deserve to feel joy.

I abandoned my parents
and failed to protect Vivi.
I'm a statue, not a human.

Arrival Stories
Dariel

Abuelo must sense Soleida's mood swings
because he responds to her request that he tell
his story of arrival in Costa Rica long ago.

The guide has left us alone,
and even though the beach
is crowded with villagers
guarding turtle nests,
I experience
a wave
of loneliness
like the vibrating
echoes I feel right after
singing.

I've heard my grandfather's story
many times, but each retelling reveals
new details.

Illegal Music
Soleida

Dariel's abuelo says his name is Trinidad,
just like the town where he was born.

He was un músico in a son montuno conjunto,
an old-fashioned band that sang love songs
instead of the government's military marches.

He refused to write lyrics about volunteering
to chop sugar cane, or fight enemies, or reject
any contact with relatives who'd left the island
and gone into exile.

So his family fled to La Habana, where they climbed
the wall of an embassy, not even sure which country
it belonged to; all he knew was that he needed to sing
the way his homemade guitarra sounded best,
a combination of horse hoofs and wingbeats,
a lullaby of love for nature's gift
of love.

Unwritten Lyrics
Dariel

Abuelo ends his tale of arrival in Costa Rica
with a little song about how grateful he was
for the peace he found in a forest.

That's a detail I've heard before,
but this time he adds just enough
of a melody
to inspire
my own
version . . .

only I don't have time
for songwriting now.

I want to hear Soleida's voice
telling her own arrival story.

Imagining the Past and Future
Soleida

I let my imagination slide backward
into that embassy, then the airplane
that brought a musician to this land
where he was allowed to sing
from his heart.

There must be some way
to bring Mami and Papi here.

Imagine the statues they would carve
with no persecution to protest!
Humans and birds would both
be able to use their own strength.
No chains.
Just wings
of growth.

Confession

Dariel

In sunlight
Soleida glows.

I almost
forget
why
I'm
here . . .

but now it's my turn
so I rush through the tale
of being chased by flames.

Walking with Poetry
Soleida

Fire must be just as terrifying
as the rising sea, but it's harder for me
to imagine, because I've always lived
in a land of rain.

I start with the statues, the hurricane,
art police, then Liana and Amado,
even including their singing dogs
just in case that Taíno-era music
is somehow related to your guitarra,
both sharing the same
island magic.

It's hard to describe how lonely I was
when I arrived in Venezuela and searched
for Vivi, but there were songbirds weaving nests
on treetops above shantytowns in Barquisimeto,
la Ciudad de la Música, where children played
orchestral instruments
to help them forget
their hunger.

When I finally found Vivi,
she was already preparing
to leave.

Venezuela had become too dangerous.
Vivi had no food, no medicine for her patients,
and no protection from thieves who robbed
the clinic even though there was nothing
left to steal.

We'll walk, she said.
So we set out on foot
and crossed into Colombia
at a place called Cúcuta
as part of a huge caravana
of caminantes, all of us
hoping to find refuge
somewhere.

Our feet froze
on the high Andean plateau,
and later, far below in the tropics,

we grew dehydrated after drinking
from streams polluted by mining.

We slept in forests, villages, coca fields,
ate whatever we could, found work
occasionally, picking roses
for bouquets that would soon
be flown to florist shops in Chicago
and New York.

Everything we owned was stolen
somewhere along the way.

No money.
No documents.

So we worked again
selling flowers on street corners.

Vivi recited poetry as we walked,
and we talked about the birds from home
and these new ones we were learning

to identify in the rain forest, toucans,
parrots, guans, and so many kinds
of hummingbirds
that I could hardly
believe my eyes,
but my favorites were the trogons,
which reminded me of tocororos,
and the macaws, both green
and red, because Vivi taught me
that los guacamayos
fall in love
and mate
for life.

Imagine putting a lovesick macaw in a cage,
she would say, you might as well hold
a human bride
captive.

Vivi wove words
the way oropéndola birds
weave teardrop-shaped nests
that resemble immense baskets

with many entrances and exits
like an apartment house
for dozens of breeding pairs
of winged marvels.

Strangers helped us.
Others chased us.

We were hundreds of caminantes,
venezolanos y cubanos,
in a country
that had no way to feed all of us,
so we fed each other
by taking turns working.

Sometimes we could afford to ride buses
instead of walking.

There were days when all we ate
was termites or squirming palm grubs.

La caravana of desperate refugees grew
to include families from Haiti, Sri Lanka, Nepal,

Cameroon, Syria, Eritrea.
There were people
from any suffering place
where no one could obtain
permission to join relatives
in California or Florida,
Texas, Baltimore,
Ohio, or far beyond
in Toronto.

Vivi and I finally had no choice
but to separate ourselves
from most of the caravan
so we could work
and save
to pay for passage
across the bay of Necoclí.

We bought a guarantee of safety
from armed men who promised to escort us
across Darién, the only truly roadless gap
in the Pan-American Highway
that runs all the way

from Argentina
to Alaska.

Everyone knows that no walker survives
in Darién
alone.

We needed to be smuggled.
We had to trust thugs
with guns, wearing camouflage,
men who tormented
all the women in our little group
of twenty-two caminantes.

Vivi's medical training helped
because she soon gained recognition
as someone the smugglers could trust
for treating viper bites, scorpion stings,
and infections from sharp palm thorns
coated with bacteria.

Rain, downpours, mudslides,
ticks, mosquitoes, fevers,

botfly eggs on my skin,
the maggots
drilling
  their way
through
  my flesh.

One night I found myself standing
face-to-face with a jaguar.

I was rescued by a local Emberá woman
who shouted, clapped her hands, and sang
a chant to chase the big cat away,
then refused to accept payment,
insisting that we
would surely do the same
for her.

Her house was a thatched haven
built on stilts, to hold her family
high above floodwaters.

We should have learned from her.
We should have waited for a time
with no storm clouds
above the dense forest,
no danger of flash floods
sweeping through canyons,
walls of water
towering . . .

but we listened to the smugglers
who promised that we had almost
reached safety, no more risk
of drowning
or being crushed
by tumbling stones
so we followed
our tricky guides
until they abandoned us
with no food
shelter
or map,

not even
a game trail
or footpath.

We could not find our way back
to the other walkers, or the Emberá village,
or any location that was not churning
with mud and stones, a flash flood
tumbling us
into depths.

Once again
just like at home
I was drowning.

This time
the water was too rough
for swimming, so I grabbed
an overhanging branch
and held on, clinging.

My position was so similar
to one of my parents' rooted sculptures

that I thought maybe I would grow wings
and escape
to rescue
Vivi
but by then
she had vanished.

I never saw her again.
No one answered my cries
for help.

I climbed
higher and higher
in the tree, but even
with a view
there was no way
to see beyond the flood.

So I waited.
Stayed awake.
Spoke to owls.
Insects.
Frogs.

When the waters finally receded
after a few hours or days—I'll never
know which—I stepped down into
the murky sludge and walked
forever.

Everything felt like geologic time,
not human.

Howler monkeys answered me at dawn
and at dusk, while in between there were
serenades by birds, but never
a single
voice
that
knew
words.

Peccaries, pumas,
a tapir, ocelots,
my footsteps
kept a rhythm

no matter which animal
watched me.

Even though I was grieving
and fearful, I danced my way
back to safety, only to discover
that being safe
did not prevent
loneliness.

First Touch
Dariel

Soleida
pauses
reaches
touches
my hand
just long enough
to take away the binoculars
I'd pulled out of my backpack
while she spoke, hoping she
might find some comfort
in those two little circles
of altered vision.

Her fingers on mine feel
like magnets.
I crumble
and shift, mind and heart
two pools of iron ore
moving toward her
silence.

Binoculars
Soleida

My story can wait.
I need this magic.

Two small circles
of magnification.

Portals for entering a realm
of aerial wonders,
all the rhythmic
whirring
pounding
wingbeats
of creatures
that peer down
while I gaze up.

A roseate spoonbill
the color of sunset.

A boat-billed heron
that looks like a cartoon.

But binoculars aren't enough distraction
to make me unaware of that instant
when my fingers and yours touched,
made contact, like alien planets
altering swift orbits,
the curiosity
overwhelming.

Instead of resting
I decide to resume speaking
so that I won't have to finish
this ordeal later.

My mouth opens
but the sound
that comes out
is more of a moan
than a story, as I describe
hearing the first hint of safety—
dogs barking, then horse hoofs,
women laughing, men shouting,
a generator, and suddenly

scent instead of sound—food:
beans, corn, manioc, plátanos.

A pregnant woman rowed me in her canoe
to a place where soldiers scanned my eyes
and recorded the patterns in the irises,
then pressed my fingertips into ink
to capture a design that resembles
tree rings.

A man asked questions
to make me speak
so he could decide
if my identity
was truly cubana.

An island accent is the only proof of origin
for someone who has no passport.

They shaved my head.
Dug out the botfly larvae.
Disinfected me.

Dressed me.
Burned my old clothes,
the only remnants of my trek
alongside Vivi, except for a few
fragments of poems that rolled around

inside my flooded mind
like nuggets of gleaming metal
that made me feel
almost real.

Everything else
seemed imaginary.

That first refugee camp was a warehouse
shared with twelve hundred other
rescued caminantes.

A cot, a blanket,
no pillow, no sleep.
Just regrets.

Then a bus, ferry, and another bus
all the way to Costa Rica.

I'd Rather Sing
Dariel

but I know you need more than music
so I take my phone from my pocket
and find your parents

freedom-of-expression groups
all over the world, with their names
on lists of persecuted artists who need
to be released by repressive governments
and given political asylum overseas

your image is online too
all over walls in Havana
as graffiti labeled LA NIÑA AVE
bird-girl

apparently those statues
inspired paintings of chained wings
in Miami, Stockholm, Paris, Madrid

you're as famous as my parents
only less recognizable, because you
are changed every time a different artist

or sculptor, or rapper, or poet
creates you

listen to all these songs about you
tocororo-girl, who cannot be caged
or defeated, or ignored

so the answer to your question
about what's next is—don't return
don't even try to go back to the island

stay here
we'll find your prima
la artista Mireya, who needs
no last name

look, here she is, in this gallery
at an opening of her landscapes

it's not very far, just up in the mountains
we'll get permission for you to live there
instead of staying in the camp

Doubt
Soleida

Just when I'm starting to believe
that you might really be able to take me
to Mireya's house, a flock of green macaws
soars by overhead, squawking cheerfully
like visitors from a happier galaxy.

Our guide returns.
Your abuelo is busy scribbling
in his notebook, but you and I
share binoculars, one eye each
looking up at a species
that falls in love
and mates
for a lifetime
of eighty years.

REFUGE

Soleida and Dariel

central mountains, Costa Rica

April 2019

The Lives of Cousins
Soleida

Mireya lives in a place
of unimaginable beauty.
We drive through a misty forest
on a dormant volcano, canyons
and waterfalls leading us to groves
of coffee planted in the shade
of native trees.

When we step into my cousin's home
the shapes of green leaves are still with us.
Everything is painted—walls, ceiling, floors.
Mireya is like a street artist who fills
her surroundings with beauty
no matter where she is.

We sit on cane rocking chairs
of the sort you find in Cuba.

I sway back and forth
as if cantering on a gentle horse.

Mireya smiles and pours coffee
from her own trees as she introduces
her husband, Alfredo, a costarricense
who tells us his name means
"wise counselor to elves,"
laughing as he shows us photos
of all the elf-like baby sloths
he has rescued.

Their daughter, Yara,
is a wildlife biology student
at the university, home on weekends,
especially this one, because she's so eager
to meet me.

As soon as we embrace
I feel like one of those orphaned
perezosos, a little sloth who needs
to be welcomed
by a substitute family.

Cloud Forest
Dariel

I don't know how Abuelo got permission
for us to bring Soleida here, driving her up
that winding road where everything is alive,
even the air, exposed roots of orchids
dangling in mist to absorb moisture.

Whatever strings were pulled
for permission from refugee camp officials,
it's worth it, just seeing Soleida
so peaceful.

We try to rent one of the cabins
near the farmhouse for ourselves,
but Mireya refuses to accept payment.

She says these cabins are free
to visiting artists, and we qualify
because of my guitar, handmade
by Abuelo.

Second Touch
Soleida

family, food, laughter,

and yet somehow all I want

is to walk around the forest with you

sharing
binoculars
one tiny circle
for each of us

our hands
   overlapping
like fluttering leaves

    or hidden
     roots

Forest Stroll
Dariel

fingers
entwine

sunlight
and mist

our voices
become smiles

air
lips
kiss

My Room Is a Forest Too
Soleida

Later
indoors
alone
surrounded by murals of trees
I remember that kiss
and our interwoven hands
like a nest
of leaves.

Are you in your cabin
writing a song about our walk
so different from the long trek
that left me silent
until I heard you
sing?

Dreaming Music
Dariel

I've had girlfriends
but no one like you.

You make me long to try
new lyrics in languages
I haven't learned yet, words
from the tongues of a breeze
after hot rain, and the moon
glowing through layers
of branches, and oxygen
as it emerges from leaves
enters our breath
veins, heart,
guitar.

Time-Greed
Soleida

Mornings are for wing watching.
We share binoculars and a bird identification book.

In the afternoons, I paint on wood or canvas,
letting my nightmares from the rising sea
emerge from the tip of a feathery brush.

What do you do while we're separate?
Do you make plans to return to your home
far away?

I have your kisses
but I want promises, too.
Time, more time, no departures
or flash floods, no more
loss.

Calendar
Dariel

I'm relaxed here, until my parents
start calling to nag me about college—they send
links to applications for Juilliard, Berklee, Yale,
USC, the New England Conservatory of Music,
the Royal Academy in London, and others
in France, Norway, Argentina, Chile . . .

They don't believe
that I might study trees
instead of symphonies.

They don't know about you
or my new schedule, a blank
page with nothing but kisses
and bird songs.

Art Flames
Soleida

Mireya asks me to stay and listen
when your abuelo interviews her
for his book about los cubanos
de Costa Rica.

She calls herself a tica cubana,
laughing because the nickname
costarricenses use for themselves
comes from the way they end words
by saying "chiquitico"
instead of "chiquitito," but that's
something islanders do too,
as if we're related
by linguistics.

Mireya's story is disturbing.
She escaped from the island
after her paintings were burned
in a bonfire
because she was a student
of Tomás Sánchez, whose style

is detailed rain forest landscapes
so green and leafy that they look real.

Far below the canopy
there is always one lone walker
on a pathway, or meditating
on the shore of a river
or the ocean.

It was 1981, the end of the gray period,
when artists were expected to follow
the Soviet style of dull colors,
huge muscles,
machetes, guns,
men conquering
enemies, including
nature.

Mireya was ordered to paint over
his canvases, and eventually she was told
she had to burn them—these commands
came from the bearded ruler himself,

so they could not be ignored
or disobeyed.

When Sánchez escaped to Costa Rica,
Mireya followed, and she says he still
lives nearby, painting his own vision
instead of military
propaganda.

Agroforestry
Dariel

Alfredo shows me how he grows coffee
in the shade of a forest that his father
replanted, after his grandfather
logged all the trees
to graze cattle.

There's only one barren pasture left now.
Everything else has been restored
so that birds and animals
once again roam
their natural habitat.

I try to picture Abuelo working here
back in the '80s, when he was a refugee.
It must have been heaven compared to
chopping sugar cane in a prison camp,
the penalty for musicians in Cuba
who sang illegal songs.

Contemplation
Soleida

Dariel and I sit beside a stream
watching birds and listening
to their voices.

Hands linked, we let our minds
wander back and forth between
the past and future, content
for now
just to be
close.

Action
Dariel

Later, awake in the cabin
while Abuelo snores,
I grab my phone
and start creating
new social media accounts—
Freedom for Artists—
in English, Spanish,
and a few other languages.

Soleida's parents deserve
a full-blown human rights campaign.

As much as I hate depending on my parents
I send them the links, knowing that by morning
other celebrities will follow, and before long
the island's art police will be so notorious
that there might be some effort
to make a few public gestures
of mercy.

Our Imaginations Rise Up and Fly
Soleida

The next day, when you show me
what you've done, I can't believe
you would stay up all night
trying to help my family.

At siesta hour, while everyone else
is resting in hammocks, you and I walk
looking at birds in the forest.

The field guide has a diagram of a feather.
Hollow shaft.
Quill.
Vane.
After-feathers.
Barbs, barbules,
hooklets.

Together, we imagine how it would feel
to trust the air to lift us
as we
kiss.

Feathery Moments
Soleida and Dariel

magnetic
shoulders
knuckles
fingertips
as we hold shared binoculars close
to witness a green honeycreeper
a golden woodpecker
and fiery-billed aracaris
that resemble toucans
dressed up for a carnival
with costumes
and dance steps

Hummingbird Names
Dariel

violet sabrewing,
blue-throated goldentail,
purple-crowned fairy,

if only I could sing
the way they fly
shimmering
for you

And Then . . .
Dariel and Soleida

We're back indoors again
urgently working
on the human rights
campaign
contacting
experts
advocates
spokespeople
for freedom-of-expression movements
all over the world—we feel so encouraged
when we learn that ordinary people
in nearly every country
all agree
that sculptors
who carve chained bird-girls
deserve to be released
from prison.

Night
Dariel

when it's finally time to rest
we have to separate

asleep
within our own nests

but in the morning
when I see you
I know

you were close to me
in dreams

your eyes
the gleam of memory
shared

Dance
Soleida

Each morning you help Alfredo
in the coffee groves, then we eat,
and after the siesta hour you mesmerize

the humid air with your guitar, bringing
a swarm of fascinated animals
        close.

Surrounded by winged beings
and four-legged, furry ones
you set la guitarra down
    to wrap your arms
        around me
        still singing
        until
we
   sway
      twirl
        so awkwardly
that laughter   follows.

I'm Not a Good Dancer
Dariel

Even though I'm Cuban by ancestry
with rhythm in my brain, I can't
shift my feet the way you do,
so you have to lead
until I learn.

Moving too slowly
is one of the reasons
       I don't always know what to say
       when I'm not inventing songs,
       but my mouth needs
       this silence
       so we
       can

             kiss.

Silent Serenade
Soleida

I can't sing
and you aren't
a dancer.

The contrast
makes us both smile.

How can we be so different
while sharing so many
wishes?

MACAWS IN LOVE

Dariel and Soleida

central mountains, Costa Rica

May 2019

Trees Lead Us
Dariel

we walk
wherever
a path
between
roots
invites
our four feet
as if we're one
animal, a mythical
centaur or Pegasus
sharing one pair
of binoculars

Wings Follow You
Soleida

a bellbird
on your cabin roof
chimes

a sunbittern at the edge of a stream
displays dazzling geometric patterns
made by orange, gold, and black feathers

y un quetzal resplandeciente
a bird so spectacular that his long wavy
iridescent green tail and wing coverts
cause us to gasp and stare—dazed.

We end up with no photo, just a memory
of shining colors as he vanishes into his nest
in the hollow trunk of a wild avocado tree,
the fruit so small and dark
that it almost looks blackened
and ashy, instead of green
and delicious.

Quetzal
Dariel

He's too magical for photographs.
His shimmering light can't be captured.

You tell me he's a trogon, a relative
of el tocororo, from a family of birds
that never survives
when caged.

If this forest is ever logged again
his entire species will disappear.

There won't be any quetzal to admire
in a fancy zoo or private aviary.

He's a symbol of freedom.
Without trees, there are no birds.

But he plants trees himself, by moving
fruit around, dropping hard seeds
in soft mud.

Paintbrush
Soleida

I can't wait to try.
Green, red, white, cobalt blue,
all the colors of a single quetzal
fly onto the walls of your cabin
where there are not yet
any murals.

But one bird is never enough.
I give him a mate, let him feed her
as she peeks out from a hollow
in the tree that now
surrounds you
as you sleep.

Promises
Dariel

We stroll beside a row of flowering shrubs
where hummingbirds and strange moths
that mimic them
hover.

It's easy to tell you
I don't plan to leave soon.

There's a university here
not too far away, in San José,
and you need to finish high school
but then you can join me.

It shouldn't be hard to get a student visa
now that you're legally allowed to live here
in Costa Rica.

After Promises
Soleida

Each hummingbird feather contains
one hundred million tiny structures
filled with bubbles of air that reflect light
in prism-like patterns, attracting the eyes
of other birds
with nameless colors
that humans
can't see.

I feel like my heart pulses
1,260 times per minute
and my wings pound 80 beats
each second, and I can fly
backward
        upside down
               sideways
          seeking sweet nectar.

I promise too—no departures
I won't swoop away and disappear
like Vivi.

Between Kisses
Dariel

Questions.
Answers.
Possibilities.
Speculation.
We already live
in a sci-fi world
of burning continents
and sinking islands
so now our hopes
are surrealistic too
each touch of lips
shadowed
    by wordless
        wishes.

Fledgling
Soleida

Hummingbirds can't walk.
Their curled feet are only adapted
for perching.

Until now, I've never experienced any moment
more thrilling than the sight of a baby zunzuncito
rising above her nest for the first time
as she discovers the purpose of wings.

That's how I feel with you at my side.
I've never imagined such exhilarating liberty
to touch, talk, move, embrace, paint . . .

but I'm terrified
by memories
that prove
how foolish
it was to believe
I could never be separated
from people I loved.

Home
Dariel

you
just you
no mansion
or nation
just arms
heart
mouth
voice

here
right
here

Guitar Magnet
Soleida

Kisses
must contain energy.
The intensity of your music multiplies.
Children come running
from nearby forest-farms
and from a village at the end
of a muddy road.

Blue morpho butterflies
troops of spider monkeys
red-capped manakins
and an arboreal porcupine
even though I know
from my long jungle trek
that el puerco espinas
is usually nocturnal
rarely awake
in daylight.

Surrounded by children and creatures
you just keep playing, not even trying
to add a few lyrics

because la guitarra
is working its own
wizardry, your fingers
the only enchantment needed
for communication beyond
ordinary language.

Habitat
Dariel

Two scarlet macaws
join the rest of the creatures.
Your cousin says she's never
seen them here, even though they once ranged
across most of the country, back in the last
century, before all the logging.

Let's establish mountain almond trees, she adds.
Then they'll stay, and we can release more birds
just like they've done on both coasts.

Almendro is an endangered species
that's not related to commercial nut crops;
it's a forest giant so valuable for logging
that it almost disappeared, but now it's protected
and Yara plans to rewild the old cattle pasture,
a final remnant of the era
when deforestation
was referred to
as progress.

We'll Help Plant
Soleida

In ten or twelve years
each seedling will be a tall tree
with a burst of purple flowers
followed by yellowish nuts.

No coffee groves in this new forest.
Just los almendros, producing abundant food
for macaws, one endangered species
supporting another.

Yara's professors will help her find birds
rescued from the illegal pet trade, but Mireya
needs to paint, and Alfredo is too busy with his crops
to do all the planting on his own, so we are the ones—
you and I, Dariel, mi cielo—we are the source of a future
for los guacamayos rojos, the scarlet macaws
that los costarricenses call lapas rojas.

So much depends on our willingness
to plunge our hands into dark
volcanic soil.

Learning
Dariel

a human rights campaign
and a reforestation project

amor at second sight
growing into more love

music waiting to be written
songs exploding from my wishes

I don't know how we'll ever manage
to do so much at once, even if we stay
awake
day and night
for a year, but
we have no choice

freedom and love
are too important
to ignore

Plans

Soleida

Trees grow slowly
but birds fly swiftly
so it's just a matter
of hope,
sweat, and years
before the new forest
becomes a wildlife refuge.

For now there are two macaws
watching and waiting, squawking,
then nesting, as if they know
they'll soon be part of a flock.

Each time you play your guitar
and sing love songs, this first pair
clings to you, huge wings resting.

They seem to trust both of us
because whenever I'm near you
they land on my shoulders,
motionless, listening . . .

The Entire Community Wants to Help
Dariel

Mireya's neighbors, the nearby town,
Yara's friends, our list of volunteers
willing to plant in June—at the height
of the rainy season—grows and grows
even though it will be years until the trees
are old enough to support a large population
of rescued birds.

Two Projects and Two Love Stories
Soleida and Dariel

Our minds flit back and forth
between the social media campaign
to free my parents and our rewilding
dream, our own amor, and the love
between these two macaws
who follow us
wherever
we go.

I've never felt so useful and hopeful
at the same time, the skin of my arms
tingling each time you sing
about
us.

The Trouble with Adults
Dariel

Everything seems perfect
until Abuelo calls my parents
and tells them I'm staying here
when he returns to Miami.

I should have sensed
this impending disaster.

Now Mom and Dad want to visit.
I know what they'll do—show up
in a four-wheel-drive limo, trailed
by fanatic fans

                    and paparazzi
                    who will spot me
                    and torment you
                    with questions
                    photos, videos
                    edited to make
                    you look slutty
                    or crazy, or both,
                    whichever sells.

Confusion

Soleida

I don't understand why you
don't want me to meet your mami
and papi. I already know your abuelo
as well as if he were my own familia.

Dariel

I should have told you
who they are
what they're like
how they travel
how you'd suffer

Soleida

Telenovela?
The one I always watched
with my own mother, both of us
all wrapped up in wild stories
of love?

Betrayal
Dariel

I'm not leaving
but Abuelo says I have to,
so I demand an explanation
and the truth is too terrible
to be anything but true.

He lied—there was no permit.
You weren't supposed to live
outside the refugee camp.

He lied to me
and to Mireya
and to you.

Now we really do have to go
so Mom and Dad won't come
and you don't need to worry
about being noticed, filmed,
questioned, and targeted
in any way that could result
in you being taken away

from your new
home.

Will you believe me
if I promise
to come back
soon?

No Forgiveness
Soleida

I can forgive the old man
for doing something he thought
would help me, but not you
for hiding who you are—
famous, wealthy,
the sort of boy
who can never
understand
me.

LOST STEPS

Soleida

central mountains, Costa Rica

summer 2019

Solitude

It's not the same as loneliness.
I watch our two scarlet macaws
enjoy their freedom to love,
mate, squawk, and eat
all the fruit and nuts
I leave out in the forest
for them to find.

I don't give them names.
They're wild.
No cage.

At night
I stay up late
painting them from memory,
not photographs.
Red body and tail,
blue-and-yellow wings—
I can't believe
they didn't vanish
along with the music
that attracted them
to you.

Your Music

was like those nameless hummingbird colors
that only other birds can see

without your love songs I don't even try to dream
of any future for myself; all I need is my hands
in deep volcanic soil, planting rare trees
that will feed an endangered species
while releasing
oxygen
I can breathe
and absorbing carbon
to cool the air above Earth
taming rogue
        seasons
   of floods
and flames

at home on the island all our soil was limestone
made from the shells of ancient sea creatures
but here it is lava that hardened and then
crumbled, just like
my heart

When I Can't Sleep

I get up to read books from Cuba
that I find in my cousin's library.

Imagine having an entire room
for nothing but verses and stories!

All Vivi's favorites are here,
the volumes she quoted as we walked
through our fear—José Martí,
Gertrudis Gómez de Avellaneda,
Juan Francisco Manzano,
and Dulce María Loynaz,
this last my favorite, because
she wrote a poem of joy called
"En mi verso soy libre," about feeling free
inside her own poetry.

I read, then reread *Los pasos perdidos*,
a novel by Alejo Carpentier, a Cuban musicologist
who wrote about exploring Venezuela's rain forest
in search of the origins of musical instruments.
It's a tale of love, loss, gain, and loss again,

in a place where music feels timeless
just like your mysterious guitarra
with its inexplicable magnetism.

I move through the library
like a phantom, selecting
Costa Rican poets—Carmen Naranjo,
Eunice Odio, and Yamilka No, a tica cubana
who publishes in Italy.

Ari Tison is my favorite, a Bribri
from the Caribbean coast near Panama,
but she lives in Minnesota, as if places
can be carried with us: my Cuba here,
her tropical forest there
in snow.

Jorge DeBravo's poem called "Prodigio"
seems like it was written especially for me.
It's about a walker who journeys without a path
and without knowing the destination
or the distance.

You and I

never understood each other's lives
          we share
island attitudes
                             isolated

you and I were
          a fantasy

tú y yo
             separated by an ocean
of history

now   you call   text   send videos
apologies
     love songs

but no   tú y yo
                can't find each other
we've lost our way
               of being together
even when you sing   and I wish
forever

Binocular Vision

You left these lenses that we used to share
one lens apiece, fingers twining as eyes
followed wings.

Now I go out alone to watch yellow-naped parrots
a motmot with tail feathers that resemble arrowheads
and a cotinga the same deep turquoise hue
as your eyes.

Alone
I listen to the melody
of a ruddy-capped nightingale thrush
and the rhythm of a cinnamon woodpecker.

Later, from memory
I paint kingfishers, quail doves,
a cayenne squirrel cuckoo, vireos,
a glow-throated hummingbird,
and Costa Rica's national pájaro—
the clay-colored thrush, so modest
and subtle in this land of exhilarating
rainbow-hued feathers

that aren't really
any more beautiful
than the thrush, who looks
like he was fashioned from
Earth, from
fertile
mud.

Almost and Always

I paint both storms
swirling hurricane waves
and a towering wall of flash flood
sorrow.

I paint un tocororo
y la guitarra
and you.

I paint my fingertips   reaching to meet yours
in midair   almost   love

Then I return to my new purpose in life
planting almendro trees, one at a time
until I've rewilded an entire forest.

I dodge venomous snakes, avoid biting ants,
endure mosquitoes, discover strength,
forget doubts, devote my hands and mind
to a pair of macaws that can live eighty years
always   always   always   in love.

DISTANCE

Dariel

Florida and Cuba

summer 2019

Miami

airport
paparazzi
cameras
questions

no wonder Abuelo made me leave you
if these scavengers had seen you
they would have swallowed us
attracting the official attention
of authorities who could send you
back to a tent in a remote camp

but I'm still angry with everyone
who made it impossible for us
to stay together
without being noticed

Abuelo
my parents
strangers

none of them matter—only you

Guitar Fury

alone with Abuelo
in his nostalgic Cuban-style Miami house
I pick up my guitar and turn it into a drum

so
much
rage
that
I
pound
this beautiful wood
palm   fists
any part
of my hand that ever
believed in possibilities
music, future, love
bruised fingers
broken strings
scars

Omen?

asleep
    feathers
        cascade
           over
               me
a waterfall
    of shattered
        songs

are we trading dreams?
        do you see flames
and a tangle
            of unraveling
guitar strings?

Keepsake

In the morning
my memory of feathers
in a dream
is tied to my guitar strap
even though the plumes
are invisible.

Guitar Frenzy

Abuelo watches me struggle
                    to tune the guitar
while I'm so confused and upset
                    that my hands
are like drumsticks
                    strings
                            keep
                                    breaking.

I might as well listen to old stories instead.
Abuelo tells me for the thousandth time
how he cut this island wood himself
and shaped the instrument
so he could serenade the girl
who became
my abuela.

It's a box of air and time, he explains
una caja de aire y tiempo that has always
been miraculous
like love.

Air and Time

Abuelo's story about how he fell in love
all those decades ago
makes me think in a different way
about this moment
right now
when I should be helping you
somehow
instead of just writhing around
in self-pity.

Your parents—the human rights campaign!
I'll get busy and circulate more petitions, direct
all sorts of celebrities to our online info
about freeing artists who protested
the censorship of art.

I check social media—plenty of images
from Havana, new tocororo-girl street art
pops up every night
inspired
by you.

At First You Don't Answer . . .

but I keep writing, calling, sending songs
across the sea, until finally I begin to receive
photos of paintings
storms
guitar
our hands

you're really good
an artist who knows how to paint
inside my mind

no words
just visual images

so I answer with music
my only true language

Homeland of Life

Abuelo is the one who suggests that we
visit Cuba, so close and yet—until now—
completely unimaginable.
It's so complicated.
Special visas.
Travel restrictions.
A bit of rejection to help me
see how it feels when refugees
are turned away by the United States
and so many other countries.

A few relentless paparazzi follow me,
still trying to figure out why I'm here,
where I'm going, and when I am going
back to California, don't I want to perform
like my parents, will I join their telenovela
or the superhero movie, why don't I try
a musical show in Las Vegas, sing
to dangerous wild animals, maybe
wolves, teach them to howl . . .

Those questions are half the reason I decide
to forgive Abuelo just long enough
for us to get along during our pilgrimage
to his birthplace, where he plans
to scatter
Abuela's
ashes.

Landing in Havana

It's emotional.
Abuelo cries.
I sort of choke
and fall silent
when ordinarily
I might hum
or sing quietly.

By the time
we're out
of the plane
I know
my plan.

Artists.
Galleries.
Back alleys.
Graffiti.

I'll search
until I find
useful clues.

Secret Art

The shock of crumbling buildings
contrasts with hidden studios
on rooftops and in courtyards
where artists use house paint
or chalk, or hair dye, whatever
they can find that helps them
decorate their world
of poverty.

Abuelo knows enough old folks
to find ways of asking questions
that can't be answered easily.

Las damas de blanco.
That's the answer.
Your mother
is now one
of the women
in white!

Your father isn't out of prison yet.
Even with our human rights campaign

the government isn't willing to set
both of them free at the same time.

So we go to the plaza and sit with her.
We tell her our story, your story, Vivi's . . .

She gives me a flower for you.
When I get back to someplace
with a stronger signal, I'll send videos,
but for now here's a message—stay
where you are, trust Mireya,
don't try to keep walking
don't trust
any borders
never try to cross
you could get deported.

Your mother says study
go to school, work hard
at whatever you love
never let anyone
stop you.

Muse

From Havana, we traveled to Trinidad
where Abuelo introduces me to hundreds
of cousins, all of them musical
in unusual ways.

In la plaza central there's a statue
of Terpsichore, the musa of choral music
and dance.

So these are my origins.
Cobblestone streets.
Men on horseback.
Women walking.
Children dancing.
Time travel.
Family.
The rhythms
of hoofbeats
footsteps
drums
maracas.

THE FOREST OF WALKERS

central mountains and
Pacific coast, Costa Rica

Soleida and Dariel

September 2019

Reunited
Soleida

You arrive in disguise
wearing your abuelo's clothing
a loose guayabera shirt
old-man trousers
and a soft felt hat
that makes you look
like a jazz musician
from long ago.

My arms enclose you
even though I don't know
if I'll be able to trust you.

When you left
I struggled to forget
this magnet between us
but now the pull is even stronger
like gravity
or tides.

Respiration
Dariel

I inhale your scent and your breath.
I'm like my guitar, a vessel for air.

Rewilding My Mind
Soleida

I tell you that your disguise is not needed.
I have permission now, thanks to Mireya
and Alfredo, both so persistent that officials
gave up and let me stay with them, at least
until some other country offers asylum.

So let the paparazzi follow you
as much as they want; their cameras
can't hurt me.

I'm in school. I have friends—costarricenses
who are helping me plant almendro trees
for the macaws that came to hear your music
and for all the ones we'll release later,
captive birds that are ready to be wild.

We can become ourselves again, you and I,
Dariel, just like those macaws.
We can be in love with love,
but we need a whole forest
to support us. We need a habitat
with deep roots.

Petals

Dariel

I fall silent, trying to decide whether this is the right time
to tell you that Abuelo decided to stay in Cuba
to carve more of his magical guitars.

First, I need to give you the dried flower,
a silent message
from your mother.

The blossom is una mariposa, a butterfly ginger,
Cuba's national flower, and even without words
it's a story
about wings
that are fragile—just imagine a butterfly's
courage when it flies
in wind.

Facing Our Future
Soleida and Dariel

courage
it's a word
worthy of entire
dictionaries

so many ways
to be brave

some of them
silent

Celestial
Soleida

arms
   lips
      gravity
         tides
            we fall in love
         all over again
      plummeting

orbiting

      lunar

         solar

reflected light
shared
warmth

wordless
closeness

Earthly
Dariel

We sit in the library with Mireya
and Alfredo, Yara, and an orphaned sloth
named Bienvenida, a baby they rescued
after her mother was electrocuted
by climbing on power lines.

Everyone questions me.
Why did Abuelo stay in Cuba?
How can we help las damas de blanco
and the prisoners?

How long will I be here?
Am I willing to climb trees
and help Alfredo string up ropes
across roads so sloths won't climb
power lines, where they get electrocuted?

A lesson follows, about three-fingered
versus two-fingered species of perezosos.
Bienvenida is the former, with three long
clawlike nails on each hand
and a need for native leaves and flowers

to eat, unable to adapt to a diet of foreign
vegetables like the two-fingered species,
the only one that can be kept in zoos.

If three-fingered sloths don't live
in wild forests, they won't survive at all.

Por supuesto I say yes to everything,
volunteer work creating rope bridges,
and later, in the fall, when coffee berries
are ripe, I'll help with the harvest.

I can't say the rest out loud
in front of everyone
so I just hum
under my breath
hoping you'll hear
island music
and understand.

No More Questions
Soleida

I don't ask you anything.
I don't need forever.
Not anymore.
I'm my rooted self again.
Strong enough to wait
for answers
that grow
slowly
like trees
in a forest
dedicated
to walkers
and winged
beings.

Rope Bridges
Dariel

Alfredo and I rappel alongside ceibas,
wild fig trees, and other tropical giants,
carrying cables to string up a highway
of aerial lines that sloths can use
to safely cross farm roads without
getting electrocuted.

Each branch drips with mosses,
lichens, bromeliads, and orchids.

I feel like I've been lifted
up into a world of illusions.
Stick insects imitate twigs.
Snakes look like vines.
Flowers mimic wasps.
Potoo birds resemble
peeling bark.
Thorns are filled
with stinging ants.
Butterfly wings
stare at me
with owl eyes.

All I need now
is a way to transform
this experience of height
and heightened attention
into a melody
of hope.

Imaginary Smiles
Soleida

While you're in the treetops
I plant almendros, then paint
my mother in the plaza
dressed in white
holding white flowers
dreaming of my father
in a place I can't picture
without seeing rats
and cockroaches
instead of blossoms.

Will artists ever be safe in Cuba?
What about an old man who carves
magical guitars? Can he create
those musical instruments
without being noticed
by the secret police?

I try to paint the orphaned sloth
but she keeps smiling, and I know
it's not real.

Perezosos don't have the right facial muscles
for changing their expressions.
All they have is permanent markings
that resemble
smiles.

So I paint her the way she is:
young and vulnerable in a world
full of predators.

Brave Art
Dariel

You paint me singing to Bienvenida.
Then you paint my guitar playing by itself
in midair.

You paint our pair of macaws in love
landing on my shoulders, while my arms
enclose you.

You paint your parents
together again
winged
and rooted
sculpted
on treetops.

Winged Walkers
Soleida

los caminantes
walk through this farm
all the time

people
just like me
from countries
just like mine

we feed them
and give them boots
the one thing every walker needs
even more desperately
than poetry with a rhythm
of wingbeats
and footsteps.

Invitation
Dariel and Soleida

Yara arranges for both of us to speak
in a climate migration session at a youth
climate action conference
in the capital city of San José
next month.

How will we prepare?
One of us is rich and fled from a fire
that did not care about money.

The other is poor
and escaped from a sinking beach
on an island where the climate crisis
is just one of so many other more urgent
reasons to flee.

TIME TRAVEL

Soleida and Dariel

Pacific coast, Costa Rica

October 2019

Visions
Soleida

ideas
flash
appear
vanish

my parents
their sculptures
myself as a statue
hidden under waves
the rising sea

Mami with her pale flowers   protesting
Papi in his prison cell   waiting
Vivi, her poems carved on clouds
syllables
falling
as rain
a mist
of wishes

you running from flames
me
walking
forever

macaws
in treetops

our new lives
your music

my wingbeats
a rhythm

our future
no homeland
just life

Parents
Dariel

Just when I begin to feel
truly independent, Mom and Dad show up
in a quiet electric car, alone, no chauffeur
or paparazzi, no adoring or creepy fans.

Mom looks so different without makeup.
She hugs me and gives me a stack of papers—
Abuelo's interviews of Cuban refugees
in Costa Rica.

He's too busy to do it himself, Dad explains
with sad eyes, but we both know that's not true.
Abuelo chose to give up his freedom to write
as soon as he moved back to his homeland
for a life of music
without lyrics.

He wants me to finish his book.
I nod.
Then search
for you.

How carefully you approach.
Are you afraid of rejection?

Mom hugs you.
Dad smiles.

They stay just long enough
to admire Mireya's paintings
and yours.

They don't ask me to sing
or nag me about college.

By the time they're ready to leave
I feel like I'm dreaming.

They say I'm free to study whatever I want
anywhere I choose, even here at the national
university of Costa Rica—it won't be hard
for me to get a student visa in the country
where my father spent most
of his childhood.

College Dreams
Soleida

Mireya says I can get a student visa too.
She'll help me sell paintings, maybe
even have an exhibit. . . .

She doesn't tell me
what to study.

Art?
Wildlife rescue?
International relations
    so I can help other
caminantes
    find refuge?

When We're Alone
Dariel and Soleida

we speak
of college

or sometimes
we don't talk at all
just touch, taste, inhale,
embrace, entwine
like winding strands
of imagination

when we're alone
we're not alone

together forever
is a time-travel fantasy
but we accept it because
years aren't always enough
we need centuries
of love

A Glimpse of the Future
Soleida

Yara invites us to visit a reforestation project
on the Nicoya Peninsula in Guanacaste Province
where mountain almond trees have been planted
so that scarlet macaws can be released
without starving.

It's a chance to see what our own new forest
will look like in a few years.

At the macaw rescue center
we watch as young birds
practice cracking hard shells
to extract nutmeats
with their tough tongues.

One guacamayo tries to steal from another
and is rebuffed with a sideways kick
and a smirk that almost looks human.

Researchers explain all the details
of rearing featherless hatchlings

to become dark-eyed juveniles,
then later adults with shining
yellow eyes that look like gold.

The release of a breeding pair
is the highlight of our day.

Flying with raucous calls
and triumphant wingbeats
the brilliant creatures
reach their new forest
and disappear
into green.

A Glimpse of the Past
Dariel

After the breathtaking sight
of captive birds claiming liberty
we drive to a place that is sacred
to all Cubans.

Here on this coast in 1893
José Martí the poet visited Antonio Maceo
the rebel general who had to flee the island
after two failed wars for independence
from Spain.

Costa Rica had gained its own freedom
half a century earlier and actively supported
the island's struggle, offering a farm as a refuge
for Maceo and his soldiers.

Just a few years after that peaceful meeting
between the poet and the general, another war
defeated Spain, and the colonial era ended.
Now, as we picnic overlooking the historic
farmland, it occurs to me that I need to add
a preface to Abuelo's book

about los cubanos
refugiados en Costa Rica.

My grandfather's
generation was not the first.
They followed Maceo
and Martí.

A Love Song for This Moment
Soleida

So many birds and creatures join your voice
the next time you sing, that the shadows
of feathers
feel like a cool breeze
as your fire-scarred fingers
drum against the guitar
filled with air from the land
of our ancestors.

Each verse is more enchanting than the last,
each audience of migrating tanagers, cardinals,
and orioles more colorful as I paint you
with songbirds resting
on your arms,
a friendship with wildness
that keeps growing, as winged beings
add their own melodies
to your lyrics
of love.

A LOVE SONG FOR THE FUTURE

Dariel and Soleida

San José, Costa Rica

October 2019

The Youth Climate Action Conference
Dariel

Three days.
Hundreds of speakers.
Thousands of listeners.
One hundred countries.
A goal of net-zero carbon emissions
by 2040.

Imagine the consequences
if we don't succeed.

We're more interested in hearing
about reforestation than dwelling
on dire predictions, so we listen to sessions
about Costa Rica as a role model, doubling
its forested area in only thirty years
by banning logging
ending cattle subsidies
and offering tree-planting
financial incentives to farmers.

Vocabulary
Soleida

green energy
blue carbon

conservation
cooperation

most of it
makes sense

I search for pictures
so the numbers will be easier
for my mind to absorb

diagrams of photosynthesis
the carbon cycle, only half a trillion
more trees are needed to slow climate change
by 25 percent

but 80 percent of plants and animals live
in existing forests, so it's logical to protect
them from deforestation

Songs and Pictures
Dariel and Soleida

Can we cool Madre Tierra
with music and paintings?

Yes, if they inspire others
to join tree-planting projects
or become scientists who can solve
complex problems.

Timeline
Dariel

There's a poster session
where I find Abuelo's birthdate
on a calendar—1951.

During the sixty-eight years of his life,
the average atmospheric carbon dioxide
has risen from 300 parts per million
to 419, an increase so rapid
that for the first time
I truly realize
that the word
"unsustainable"
is terrifying.

The world needs to hurry.
Old lawmakers need to let young people
help make decisions, because we'll be
the ones who will still be alive
at the end of this century
when so many countries
might already
be uninhabitable.

The Maldives are sinking now.
Kiribati Island is almost submerged.
The population is already
being relocated to Fiji.

There will be 143 million climate migrants
by 2050.

Right now there are already 24 million
per year.

We need hope.
Optimism.
Action.
Now.

The Future Is Leafy
Dariel and Soleida

After a session by Indigenous teenagers
from North, Central, and South America
we dry our tears.

A Métis girl from Canada asked the audience
what sort of ancestors we want to be.

Both of us whispered our answer to each other—
ancestors who planted trees.

Our Turn to Speak
Soleida and Dariel

We rise together
climb a few stairs
onto a stage
that faces
an audience
of teenagers
from all over
Earth.

We speak
in alternating
voices.

Storm.
Fire.
Walking.
Flying.
Songs.
Paintings.
Macaws in love.
Endangered tree seedlings.
A new forest.

Our minds
rewilded.
Our courage
growing.

We're just
getting started.

College is next.
Then much more.

We're walkers
still imagining
how to soar.

AUTHOR'S NOTE

Wings in the Wild is fiction, but most of the situations depicted are factual. Islands are sinking, and forests are burning.

Each year, tens of thousands of Cuban refugees walk to the US border from South America. Many die or vanish in the roadless Darién Gap of southern Panama. In 2018, at least eight thousand of these caminantes (walkers) were stranded in refugee camps in Costa Rica when Nicaragua refused to let them pass. In 2020, they were finally given permission to stay and work in Costa Rica while seeking permanent asylum.

In November 2021, Nicaragua began allowing Cubans to fly in without a visa, resulting in a much shorter overland journey. By September 2022, more than two hundred thousand Cubans had fled the island, walking from Nicaragua to the US border. It became the largest exodus since the 1960s, amounting to one percent of the entire population of Cuba.

Like Dariel's abuelo, some of my own Cuban relatives found a refuge in Costa Rica much earlier, during the 1980s. Like Dariel, I live in California, enduring the constant fear of wildfires intensified by the climate crisis. Like Soleida, I am the child of artists, and I love birds.

Artists, poets, and musicians in Cuba have been censored for decades, but in 2018, Ley Decree 349 entrenched the criminalization of dissident art in the new constitution. Persecution of artists has been so drastic that on July 11, 2021, island-wide protests were sparked by the beating, arrest, and disappearance of hundreds of artists, rappers, poets, journalists, and bloggers. One month later, Ley 35 made it illegal to report any negative events on social media, classifying complaints as cyberterrorism.

Other factual aspects of this novel occurred even earlier. Antonio Maceo really was granted asylum in Costa Rica, and José Martí visited him there in 1893, expressing gratitude for Costa Rica's active support of Cuba's struggle for independence from Spain.

Costa Rica is now a model for climate action. Reforestation projects have doubled the forested area in thirty years.

In October 2019 scarlet macaws were released in a mountain almond reforestation project on the Nicoya Peninsula, and a youth climate action conference met in San José.

Macaws really do fall in love and mate for life. Just like humans, they can live eighty years.

Tocororos in Cuba and quetzals in Costa Rica are related species. Neither can be caged. They die in captivity.

Costa Rica is home to Tomás Sánchez, the most successful of Cuba's living artists. His stunning paintings really were burned by Fidel Castro as punishment for the way the artist depicted humans as smaller than trees at a time when Soviet influence demanded images of powerful men conquering nature.

During a series of visits to Costa Rica beginning in 1980, I have been blessed with a chance to see quetzals, scarlet macaws, sea turtle nests, and rescued sloths. I am grateful to the people of Costa Rica for offering refuge to Cubans and for serving as a global model for nonviolence, reforestation, and the protection of existing forests. If the rest of us follow their example, we will be able to help slow the devastation of climate change.

I am indebted to Métis author Katherena Vermette for the question "What sort of ancestor do you want to be?" When I heard her ask this at a conference, I knew the answer would inspire me for the rest of my life. I want to be an ancestor who planted trees.

Margarita Engle
botanist, agronomist, and poet
California
August 2021

ACKNOWLEDGMENTS

I thank God for hope.

I'm grateful to environmentalists all over the world, and to human rights organizations working to free imprisoned artists, writers, and musicians in Cuba. I'm grateful to anyone who helps climate migrants and other refugees.

In Costa Rica, I'm grateful to the Sloth Institute, the Macaw Recovery Network, Kids Saving the Rainforest, Monteverde Cloud Forest Biological Preserve, and Sea Turtle Conservancy.

I'm grateful to my family, especially my husband, Curtis Engle, who always plants trees wherever we live. Special thanks to my agent, Michelle Humphrey; my editor, Reka Simonsen; our art director, Rebecca Syracuse; our cover artist, Gaby D'Alessandro; and the entire publishing team.